What Goes

Around

A lost hubcap. A flea market. You get what you bargain

for.

K.S.P. PLAHA

ISBN: 978-1-990496-75-2

Cover Design:

Visit AOS Publishing's website:

www.aospublishing.com

Start of play

At the start of his retirement, a theft was not something Devansh Patil was looking forward to. In fact, as he emerged from his bedroom with a prayer thali, he was blissfully oblivious to it. The fragrance from the incense sticks on the venerated steel dish was caught in the whirlpool of air from the ceiling fan, and it soon filled the living room. He walked with practised ease towards the altar adorned with an impressive image of Lord Shiva. There, he bowed with folded hands for several moments.

Fondly known as *Dev* to friends and family, he had worked the 9-to-5 grind for over four decades. After receiving a decent severance pay, one of the first things Dev allowed himself was a brand new car: the Opel Astra. To it, he had

added custom wheel trims of the Ferrari 360 series. Right

this moment, his pride and

joy was parked on the street, not too far from the main gate

of the building complex where he lived—albeit missing

some of its bling. As Dev would soon find out, not

everyone had retired: not least the thieves.

Almost a month into his retirement, he was looking

forward to a road trip with his wife to Goa. If all went well,

and the Gods smiled down on him, that would be a good

start to his journey of rest and retreat. As an immediate

recreation, he was excited about the cricket test series,

between India and Australia, which was about to

commence in less than an hour. One pleasure that

retirement allowed him was being able to watch all the

games; each five days long. The television and the couch would be his arena for the next few weeks.

He finished the prayers and called out to his wife:

"Urmi, I'm hungry. Breakfast please!"

"It will go cold on the table, if you delay any longer!"

"Thanks my dear. And don't forget to start packing for the trip. We leave early in the morning on Saturday to beat the traffic."

Urmi smiled.

"It's only Monday, you know!"

"How would I know? It's not as if I have to catch a train to work," Dev replied with a snicker.

Urmi said nothing. The household was getting used to him parroting about his retirement.

Dev made his way to the dining table and took a careful sip from the steaming cup of tea. Then, he dove into his breakfast while his wife rushed between the kitchen, the bedroom, and the bathroom.

"Oh God!" she exclaimed to nobody in particular, "I hope I'm not late for my hot yoga class ... again!"

"Nothing can delay you, Urmi. Anyway, at the speed you're zooming around, do you really need yoga?" Dev teased and sighed with contentment.

It was at that moment that one of the kids from the neighbourhood came at the door and said:

"Uncle, uncle! Someone stole a wheel cover from your new car!"

A controversial run-out

Dev lost all appetite and charged out of the house, barefoot. He skipped down the three steps from the front door and raced to the main gate of the building compound. As a reflex, the security guard on duty stood up to help, but Dev was already on the footpath by then. There he turned right and strode to his brand new Opel Astra that was wedged between another sedan and a couple of motorbikes parked rather precariously.

Fearing the worst, he began to walk around the car, examining each tire. It was the driver's side front wheel that had its trim and hubcap missing. For a few moments, Dev stood staring at it, stunned. The colour drained from his face and then brimmed over to crimson as his body shook violently.

"O Shiva!", he cried out to the Lord, his hands raised to the sky, "Why me? Why now?"

The narrow street had all sorts of vehicles parked, with not much to spare. Some kids were setting up stumps at the end of the cul-de-sac, ready to welcome the cricket season.

"Hey kids! Do you know who did this?", he shouted out while stabbing his finger at the naked wheel, knowing fully well that it was a rhetoric. Surely, nobody was around when the theft occurred.

Some shrugs and indifference later, he made his way back to the complex gate, muttering.

"No, no, no!"

"*Saheb*, what happened?", The security guard, who had been watching him, asked with empathy. He used "Saheb" as a title of respect, a relic of the erstwhile British rule.

"What happened? Huh? What *happened*?", Dev glared at the man, "are you asking *me* what happened? What were *you* doing all night? Had a good snooze, did ya?"

"*Saheb*, I came in only at 6:00 am.", pleaded the guard in a feeble

voice, folding his hands.

"You guys are all useless! Completely!" Dev all but shoved the man aside and made his way back to his apartment. At the door steps, he bumped into his wife.

"What's the hurry, Dev?" Urmi barely managed to steady herself.

"I could ask you the same thing, no?" Dev snapped back, "Guess what? Someone stole one of the wheel trim with its hubcap!"

"Oh no ... so sorry! The special ones with the Ferrari logo?"

"Ya ...", Dev's voice trailed off.

"Now what will you do? Ask the watchman maybe …"

"Already did!", Dev cut her short, "He started his shift at

6:00 am."

"Then ask the night watchman!", Urmi suggested and then

added quickly, "I really have to go, okay? Bye."

"Yeah, yeah, Bye! Don't miss your yoga class for anything

in the world!"

Urmi ignored the sarcasm and, instead, took it as a cue to

leave. She rushed out the gate.

Back in the living room, Dev went straight to the

telephone. There he dialled the security agency's number,

each digit spinning back to its place with an ominous

stutter. When the call was answered, he skipped the

pleasantries:

"Who was the night watchman at Seva Sadan Society

yesterday … err I mean last night?"

"Sorry Sir, I'm not sure", replied the operator, "But I can connect you to the boss."

Dev repeated the question to the agency owner once the call was transferred.

"It was Subhash,"came the reply, "but may I know what the problem is? My boys never drink on the job and sure as hell, don't sleep."

"We'll see about that! One of the wheel trim has been stolen from my car. What was the watchman doing all night?"

"Hold on, hold on, *Saheb*! Where was your car parked? Inside the compound or outside on the street?"

"Why?"

"The guards are posted inside the main gate of the complex. They cannot mind the street. At least not as part of their regular duty. Anyway, that alley is so full of vehicles ...”

“How ... how does that matter?”, Dev’s impatience cut the other party off.

“Well, it’s hard for anyone to tell what’s going on, especially at night!”

After a brief pause, Dev stammered:

“But surely he would’ve noticed if someone walked away with a whole wheel cover?”

“Not necessarily, *Saheb*. After all, visibility is not that great at night. The street lights are dim and often blown. Moreover, the guard cannot question any random person walking on the street. They are not cops, remember?”

“True, true”, Dev agreed, “Not that the cops are much use these days, are they?”. There was no comment from the other end.

Dev decided it was futile to pursue the conversation. He

dropped the receiver on its cradle, and himself on the sofa.

He had been looking forward to the cricket due to start any minute. That plan had been ruined too.

Just then, his son Ganesh came sauntering into the room, cheerful and fresh.

"Hey Dad, good morning!", he greeted.

"What's so good about it, son?" Dev's tone of dejection made his son pause.

"What happened now? Is everything okay? I see you haven't even finished breakfast."

"Haven't you heard? Some creep stole a wheel trim and the hubcap along with it."

"No, not the Ferrari ones! Oh Shi—", Ganesh said, "Have you reported it to the cops yet?"

"Cops? You must be joking! They will forever make me run laps to the station and back. Nothing will be done, and nobody will be caught. A waste of time, really!"

"How do you know that Baba?", Ganesh started wolfing down his breakfast.

"Of course I know!," asserted Dev, "This hair didn't turn grey in the midday Sun. I do know a thing or two about the system. The cops are probably hand-in-glove with the thief, I guarantee you! Your generation is too complacent to the ills of our society."

"C'mon dad ... you're being paranoid", Ganesh protested.

"Really? Everyone is so corrupt these days. Especially the public sector. Haven't you noticed the traffic cops asking for a few rupees on the sly to ignore traffic infringements? Pathetic! Almost 50 years since Independence and all we have to show for it is corruption and crime!"

Ganesh wasn't about to jump into a fruitless argument on the state of the nation, or the generation gap. So, he said:

"Okay then, at least call the Insurance Agency and file a claim."

"No use." came the answer, "That will just cause the premium to skyrocket next year! They thrive on such thefts. I almost feel they are behind most robberies. It helps their *bottom-line, you see?*"

Ganesh wasn't sure if the cops were in bed with the thieves or if the Insurance agencies were. He gave up:

"So what are you planning to do now?"

"Let's see. Not sure at the moment.", Dev replied, "Damn! Those were expensive trims!"

"Alright dad,"Ganesh had finished breakfast, "I can still catch my daily train if I leave now. Let me know your plan and call my office if you need help with anything, okay?" With that, he left before Dev could reply.

A strong partnership

By mid-morning, Dev had simmered down somewhat. He was mulling his options although the cricket match had been forgotten. He was on his second cup of tea when the telephone rang.

He walked over and snatched the receiver.

"Hello, Devansh Patil here. Who's this?"

"Oh ho, Dev *Bhai*!" Mr Singh's voice boomed at the other end. Despite himself, Dev managed to smile. Daljeet Singh always addressed him as *Bhai*, a term synonymous to Brother or, just Bro.

"How are you, Daljeet?"

"Good, good, good! Why don't you come up and watch the cricket match with me?"

Dev was keen on cricket but hadn't been in the mood to switch his own TV on. He paused for a minute and then agreed:

"Okay, I'll join you in a few minutes".

"That's fantastic! See you then."

Daljeet Singh lived on the first floor, directly above his flat. Exactly ten minutes later, Dev rang Daljeet's doorbell, who was at the door at once:

"Come in, come in, fellow retiree", Daljeet beamed, "Gavaskar has just faced Dennis Lillee's first ball."

"Great, I didn't miss much then" Dev added as he took a seat in front of the colour TV, admiring it with envy. His own black-and-white TV was ancient in comparison.

"Wow, look at the colours," he shook his head, "Hey, are they playing in Bombay?"

Daljeet nodded. On the TV, Lillee ran in to bowl the next

ball.

At the end of the over, Daljeet turned to Dev and asked:

"So, how have you been, Dev, and how's the retirement? Welcome to the club, by the way!"

"Thanks. I've been good—until this morning, that is. Someone stole a wheel trim from my car. Just discovered it when a neighbourhood kid came with the news."

"What? Oh no! I did hear some commotion this morning but didn't realise you were robbed." Mr Singh sympathised, "There have been quite a few robberies recently. I am taking extra care to secure my own scooter when I park."

"Good for you," said Dev instinctively, "But mine's a brand new car, Daljeet! What's more? I bought special wheel trims and hubcaps — Ferrari ones!"

"Yeah, I had noticed. Flashy and all. Must've cost you a

fortune, no?"

"Yes, and that's why it's so frustrating that someone

decides to steal them. It may cost me another fortune to

replace them, you know?"

On the TV, Gavaskar had scored a boundary. Once the

roar of the crowd had died, Daljeet asked:

"Did you call the Police? The local inspector is a friend and

may be able to fast track your complaint.", he smiled.

"No Daljeet *bhai*. You know how I feel about the cops—

and the Law, in general" Dev replied and then added

quickly, "and same with the Car Insurance guys!"

"So true. Most of them are unscrupulous. Just like the

politicians, aren't they? Who elects these idiots?"

Dev said:

"Ah, don't get me started on our leaders, Daljeet!"

"Anyway, forget them. What's your plan now, about the

wheel trim? I'm sure the car looks horrible with one wheel so bare."

"It does, yes. I'm really not sure what to do, Daljeet" Dev said quietly, "My road-trip is ruined too. I was supposed to drive up to Goa this weekend."

"Yeah," agreed his friend, "It would be a shame to drive a brand new car in this state, with a missing wheel cap. You need a solution ... and fast!"

Dev nodded but did not offer any response. They watched the cricket in silence for several minutes.

When Daljeet's wife walked in with two cups of steaming *chai*, he exclaimed:

"Ah nice! Cricket and *chai*! Let the tea lubricate my brain cells so I can think about your problem. Don't worry!"

Mr. Patil smiled and took a sip of the tea as Indian openers had already chalked up an impressive partnership on the scoreboard.

When his wife left the room, Daljeet shuffled up to Dev and lowered his voice.

"I have a brilliant idea but I'm not sure how you'll feel about it. It is inexpensive and almost guaranteed to get you what you need. Today itself!"

Dev knew Daljeet was streetwise and had some quick-fix up his sleeve for every problem.

"Sure, tell me.", he leaned forward.

"I say you go and look for a replacement wheel trim at the *Chor Bazaar*!", Daljeet's voice was almost a whisper.

"You mean the flea market? Isn't that a haven for thieves? I have yet to hear anything good about it, Daljeet!"

"Oh no no no no! Those are urban legends. Don't believe them." Daljeet rested one hand on Dev's shoulder:

"Dev, people have bought rare items that have made them

millionaires. The vendors are often unaware of the true value of their wares. Priceless paintings worth thousands, even millions, for a few rupees! Rough diamonds, vintage items, antiques. You name it and you can find it there. Maybe even God!". He laughed raucously.

"All I want is a replacement wheel trim, thank you. But will they have the Ferrari parts too?"

"Why not? You may find your own stolen piece itself!", Daljeet was excited, "I say you get yourself to that Bazaar, my friend, and explore. For all you know, they may even install the wheel cover for you. They do have some expert mechanics around. So I've heard!"

Dev wasn't convinced but he nodded and smiled:

"Okay, let me think about it."

A huge roar went up on the TV. India's star batsman, Gavaskar, had been caught in the slips.

Post Lunch Session

Over lunch, Dev shared the plan with his wife. Urmi was unconvinced.

"I hope you don't lose more than you hope to gain," she warned him, "Remember that toaster you had 'won' at the raffle last year? The lottery ticket cost us more than that junk was worth!"

"It's not the same thing, Urmi. I am not giving a single paisa away until the wheel cover is replaced with the original one. Anyway, there's no guarantee that I'll find the same part ... that too, in one day. So, it's all a matter of chance, really!"

"That's exactly why I'm sceptical: *chance*." Urmi said with a wave of her hand.

"Alright, alright! How about I go and have a browse.

Unless I find a shop that has the exact thing at a much

reasonable price, and they are willing to replace it for me, I

won't go ahead. Does that make you feel better?"

Urmi smiled and nodded.

"Okay then, wish me luck!", Dev managed to joke.

After lunch, he was ready to embark on his expedition to

the flea market. He walked up to Lord Shiva and bowed

with folded hands for a few moments. Then, on a whim, he

called his son's office number. When Ganesh answered the

phone, he said:

"Ganesh, I spoke to Daljeet Uncle this morning ..."

"No dad", Ganesh was aware of Daljeet's dubious schemes.

"Listen," insisted Dev, "I'll drive to *Chor Bazaar* and see if

I can find the same trims. If I can get them installed as well,

that would be a bonus!"

"Bonus is not a word I would associate with that market, Dad!"

"Don't worry. I'm capable of a good bargain. Won't part with hard-earned cash without genuine parts."

"Okay, good luck dad and beware of touts! Do you want me to meet you at the market? I can take the rest of the day off ..."

"No no, don't bother. In fact, how about I pick *you* up once I'm done ... hopefully with all wheels restored to their former glory?"

"Sure dad. Why not?" Ganesh laughed.

After the call, Dev made his way to the car with determined strides. This time, the security guard decided to leave well alone.

The car gleamed in the mid-day sun and was hot to touch. He winced as he pulled the door open but avoided gazing at the naked wheel.

As he manoeuvred the vehicle out of the narrow alley and

on to a wider road, the air-con revived his spirits somewhat.

He even began to sing along to the radio.

In Mumbai, a journey between any two points can seem

like an eternity. A traffic snarl could last for hours. A

politician can decide to protest without notice or

permission. A religious procession can arrive

unannounced. Luckily, none of these calamities befell

Dev's journey which made him hopeful. Yet, when he

finally turned on to the road that led to *Chor Bazaar*, he

was apprehensive as he had never bought anything at a flea

market, always playing it safe.

"Hey, watch out!" someone bellowed and Dev slammed

the brakes. The crowd at the Bazaar was always dense. He

edged the car through a throng of people at a speed he

could easily beat if he walked. However, leaving the car and walking would be worse. The market wasn't known as *Chor Bazaar*, literally 'Thief Market', for nothing. Urban legends had claimed how a car could be stripped down to its constituent parts within the hour. He wasn't about to test their veracity and continued his arduous trip with patient apprehension.

Whenever the car came uncomfortably close to a pedestrian, they thumped it with their hand to indicate the proximity. He waded through a sea of buyers, hawkers, haphazardly parked bicycles, motorbikes, scooters and of course, cars. He was sure he spotted a Ferrari too!

"Sure that's a fake!" he muttered, "or it would've been stolen by now."

Curious eyes followed his quest. Shop vendors languished at the door, sipping tea or smoking, or both. Some haggled with their customers. It was as if nobody cared about him

and yet, everybody seemed to be watching him.

He was so busy edging his car through the crowd that he

almost missed the boy who was waving and yelling at him.

He wound the window down and the boy pushed his head

through it.

"*Saheb*, do you need a wheel cover?"

Dev wanted to yell: "Yes! Yes!!" but he was cautious:

"Where is your shop? Let me drive over to it first."

"Of course, *Saheb*. Keep edging to the right through the

crowd and you should see our popup store."

"To the wrong side of the road?"

"Do you have a choice?", the boy grinned, waving his

hands at the crowd, "You cannot possibly turn around

now, can you?"

Afternoon Tea

"Okay okay," Dev nodded and wound the window back up. The boy raced ahead, pushing through the crowd and guiding him to a popup shop. An old man wearing loose clothing and a skull cap emerged from the store.

"Yes, yes, just stop here", the man motioned to him. Dev stopped the car and got out. The makeshift store had a myriad of automobile parts but Dev could not spot the Ferrari trims.

"Do you have Ferrari trims to match these?" he pointed to his car, "I would rather not waste your time ... and mine."

"Of course, we do, *Bhai*. This is not the only shop I own here. As you can see, space is at a premium", the old man laughed, "So, I've got small pop-ups at 2-3 locations around the market."

"Ah, okay. But I would like to see the replacement parts

first."

"Of course, *Saheb*. Don't you worry. Just this morning I

was informed we have original Ferrari parts."

Dev wanted to ask if a thief had handed in one of his wheel

trim and hubcap. Then, he remembered the bright yellow

Ferrari he saw a while ago.

"Look *bhai*, I've never traded here before ..."

The vendor laughed. "I know this Bazaar is infamous,

notorious even, but some of us have been here for ages.

Not all apples are rotten, I assure you!"

Dev nodded and the old man waved him to a sofa that

looked good enough for sale too.

"Why don't you make yourself comfortable first? I am

Ahmed, by the way", he offered his hand.

Dev shook it hesitantly and said:

"Okay, before you get started, how much will it cost me?"

"Look *Saheb*," replied Ahmed, "I am an old-school guy so I believe in a fair price. How about 300 rupees?"

Dev was taken aback. The original set had cost him several thousand. He was sceptical:

"But do you have the original parts? How will I know?"

"You will know once we replace them right here, while you watch. You are, of course, welcome to examine them before we install them. Do we have a deal?"

Dev was uneasy paying the first price offered by the vendor, *any vendor*. After all, this was a flea market. He took a step back and said quietly:

"I can pay 200."

"*Saheb*, 300 is already too low, as I said—"

"200 or I can look elsewhere."

Ahmed seemed to ponder the revised offer for a few

moments and then said:

"*Saheb*, you look like a gentleman to me. Should we settle

for 250?"

"No. 200. Final."

Ahmed threw up his hands in a exaggerated gesture and

said with a sigh:

"Done. Now please sit down and be comfortable."

As Dev settled in the chair, Ahmed gestured to the same

boy who had led Dev to the shop:

"Aye Raju, fetch two cups of tea first. Then, go get the

Ferrari wheel cover from the other shop." With that he sat

himself down on a stool next to Dev's chair.

Dev's apprehension was somewhat alleviated. He could see

his car, and the wheel, from where he sat. He decided to

watch it like a hawk.

"What's happening with cricket?" Ahmed asked suddenly, "You think we'll beat Australia?"

"Hard to say. They have some of the best fast bowlers in the game. Gavaskar was out early. What's the score now, by the way?"

"Looks like we'll score 400 or more in this innings. Our middle order is strong. I'm hoping we clinch the series!"

Dev nodded. The afternoon sun was edging past the buildings as the boy arrived with tea in small glass tumblers. Handing one each to the two men, he vanished into the crowd once again.

Just then, a couple of cops strolled up to the store and yelled:

"Hey! Who owns this popup?"

Ahmed stood up: "This store is mine, Sir!"

"So far out onto the road? Is this even legal?"

Dev watched as Ahmed walked up to one of the cops and shook hands with him surreptitiously. The cop nodded and smiled. Then, they were gone.

When Ahmed was back on his perch, Dev asked:

"Bribe, eh?"

"What else, *Saheb*? This is their regular beat. Trust me, if I had asked about the legal limit for the store, they would charge me with some council offence and confiscate my wares. Then, it would be a long fight in the civil court to recover them. Losing business for days in this Bazaar can cost me a lot more."

"Understood," Dev was sympathetic, "The whole system is rotten, isn't it?"

"Honestly *Bhai*, I don't even think about it anymore," replied Ahmed with a sigh, "It's not like the old days when folks had much integrity."

"How true!" exclaimed Dev, "I am with you there Ahmed *bhai*. This country can only be saved by a strong leader—almost a dictator, I'd say." He was warming up to the vendor who seemed to be speaking his language.

"Either that or we need another revolution. Where are the Gandhi and Nehru of today, huh? People are fed up!"

Dev nodded knowingly.

Meanwhile, Raju reappeared with a set of wheel trims and hubcap and handed it to Dev, who diligently checked the logo and examined the quality of the metal. Satisfied, he nodded and smiled at the boy.

"Almost as good as mine! Go ahead. Install it."

Raju fetched a set of tools from the popup store and began installing the wheel cover. When he was done, the Sun had gone lower on the horizon and the crowd had begun to disperse.

Dev beamed at the driver's wheel with its glory restored.

He pulled out two notes of 100 rupees each and offered it

to Ahmed who accepted them and stuffed them into his

pocket.

"There you go, *Saheb*. All done! It's almost closing time

but you're welcome to another cup of tea. One for the

road, as they say!" Ahmed laughed and so did Dev.

"Another time, friend," replied Dev.

Ahmed led him to the car and even opened the door for

him, as a courtesy. As Dev settled in the driver's seat, he

had a thought.

"Do you mind if I call my son before I leave?", he asked

Ahmed.

"Of course not, *Saheb*?", said Ahmed promptly and

fetched a cordless receiver for him.

Dev dialled his son's number. When his son answered, he

smiled into the phone:

"Guess what Ganesh! I have the new trims installed already.

I should be at your office in 30 minutes ... 40 at most."

After the call, he thanked Ahmed and said:

"I just hope you didn't have to pay a hefty bribe to the

cops, earlier on."

"Ah, no need to worry, *Bhai*. We got your business too,

didn't we? What goes around, comes around!"

With that, Dev began his slow journey out of the *Chor*

Bazaar.

Close of play

Dev arrived at Ganesh's office building just as the rush hour hit. He noticed people milling out onto the streets from the offices across the block. After a while, he watched as Ganesh emerged with a bunch of colleagues, all laughing uproariously at some inside joke.

Ganesh noticed the car, which Dev imagined was hard to miss, and waved at him. Few minutes later, Ganesh crossed the road and came to greet him. He leaned back to see the new wheel cover.

""Not bad, Dad!", he waved an okay sign with his thumb and forefinger, "As good as new! I'm sorry I doubted you earlier."

"No worries. All it needed was a bit of thinking outside the square. C'mon let's go. This is a no-stopping zone!"

Ganesh walked around the front of the car to the passenger side door. He was about to open the door when he paused and then burst into a fit of laughter.

Dev was not pleased: He wound down the passenger side window and yelled:

"What's so funny now? Hurry up and get in before I get a fine for stopping illegally!"

"You must come around and see for yourself" Ganesh exclaimed, between guffaws.

Dev got out of the car and walked around.

Ahmed's last words rang true when he realised that the wheel cover from the passenger-side had been rotated around to the driver's one.

www.ingramcontent.com/pod-product-compliance
Lightning Source LLC
Chambersburg PA
CBHW071444300726
48976CB00004B/1438